Chap

The best monsters .... *in ghosts, ghouls, zombies or werewolves. Dracula? More like Hack-ula. No matter how well a story is told, how good the make-up is, how tense the soundtrack is; I know that those creatures can't exist so I never found them that scary. Jumpy, yes, but never much more.*

People, on the other hand, now they can be scary. How a human mind can stray off the beaten track so much to justify the worst acts imaginable to itself. Murder, rape, torture, mutilation. Take your pick really but to enact any against another person and not feel any remorse, empathy or guilt...that's what scares me.

"Twenty minutes, Harry" a voice called from beyond the dressing room door.

"What? Ok, yes. Thanks Jo."

"Oh and you have some fans waiting in reception."

Harry Bates had been inspecting the latex knife wound on his chest, lost in his reverie until Joanne's voice made him jump and rip the latex in the process. *God-damn jump scares, they make even a zombie shit himself.* Now he needed to go to make-up before the cameras started rolling. There was no way in hell he could see the fans before Tim called action, there was always more they wanted to do in make-up, such was their commitment to perfection. *The fans will understand...*

Four hours later, Harry towel-dried his hair after a much-needed long shower. He hadn't expected filming to have taken as long as it did, or for it be as cold as it was. He relished the moment to be warm and clean, with not a spot of blood or guts to be seen. Standing in front of the mirror he saw a slim man of just over six foot with pasty white skin. He had high cheekbones and slightly hollowed cheeks. What remained of his hair was black and patchy, fine enough to suggest it would fall out soon. To his mild annoyance he had never managed to grow more than a few smoky wisps of hair on his chin. His upper lip could produce a dark line of hair that wouldn't look out of place on a man who lurked near playgrounds in a trench coat, so that never stayed for long. His eyes were sunken in his head fractionally but noticeably. All this and his yellow-tinged, iris-less eyes gave the impression of a dying man. The shape of his skull could be easily seen, the skin stretched tight accentuating its contours. Harry smirked and reached his arms out, as if to rise from the dead himself, and pulled a snarling face.

A knock at the dressing room door broke him once again from his thoughts. Crossing the room, he opened the door to Joanne with her clipboard and headset microphone.

"Hey Harry, sorry to bother you but you've still got a fan waiting."

"I thought you didn't do horror?" She smiled and rolled her eyes.

"I don't, *he's* still in reception. The others must have left."

"Is it…"

"Oh yeah, your number one fan."

"I thought security were keeping him off-site?"

"Frank told him he could wait if he behaved himself."

"And has he?"

"Apparently so. Kept to himself and hardly brought his head up from his writing."

"Writing? Maybe he's writing his own horror film."

"You might be dying to be in his film for a change."

That made Harry chuckle. "Oh I do hope he likes my work!"

"Just a little bit."

He felt picked up after such a hard slog of an afternoon. "Oh go on then, I'll be there in a minute."

Harry had worked in the film industry for fifteen years now and had garnered somewhat of a following amongst horror fans for his work. While he didn't personally find the films scary, he understood why others did. It gave him a certain pleasure to play the monsters therein, to get bloody and gruesome, indulging a fantasy world that could not be. It felt like an escape from a world he knew too well, a release to immerse himself in the end of the world and science gone wrong. His skeletal frame and expressive face had helped him find acting work relatively easily, particularly as inhuman monsters like zombies or just downright evil people. The latter he found more interesting to play but the former offered a lot more work for a lot more money due to its current popularity, so he threw himself into it when needed. Enthusiasts of the zombie horror genre had become drawn to him as he involved himself more within that world.

Nathan Jones was one of those enthusiasts, still waiting in reception. He had entered Harry's life six months ago as a squeaky mega-fan with an omniscient ability to follow Harry's work schedule without fail. At first Harry had enjoyed the attention of such a devoted fan, however that wore off after a few weeks of sticking to Harry like a limpet. Constant questions and unerring praise had worn thin quickly, so Harry had made excuses to create distance between him and Nathan. He couldn't bring himself to give Nathan a hard push away but after a renewed fervour following Harry's latest release, Nathan had to go. It had now been three months of relative peace since security had kept Nathan off studio premises. He had waited outside for the first month but had not been seen by anyone for the past two.

Harry pushed open a heavy set of double doors and stepped into reception. A curved desk made of dark wood was on his immediate left, behind which Frank sat with a large toffee held in front of his mouth. A look of relief spread across his face once he saw Harry.

"Hey Harry" Frank said as he popped the toffee in his mouth. "You not-tss gone n-yet?" he managed with difficulty.

"Not long now. Just need to see..."

Harry looked over to the sofas across the room in the far-right corner where a man in black sat head-down, right leg over left with a notepad in hand, scribbling diligently.

"Frank, is that Nathan?" Harry whispered.

Frank nodded, still very much at work on the toffee. "hnn-didn't nyek-ognise 'im 'i-ver."

Gone was the shoulder-length mat of greasy dark brown hair, in its place was short sides with shiny, slicked-back hair on top. *He does have a forehead, who knew?* He wore a black leather jacket over a white top with black jeans and big black boots. Not a badge, pin or movie quote-embossed tee shirt in sight. *This man looks reborn.*

"Hey, err, Nathan!" Harry called over as he stepped closer. Nathan looked up and a wide smile filled his face. Gone too were the patches of dark hair usually adorning random parts of his face, he had shaved it all, apart from his thin eyebrows, and clearly lost some weight too. Nathan's face had an angular, handsome quality now, completely at odds with the pudgy, tufty and blemished face he used to have.

"Harry! Good to see you!" Nathan said warmly as he rose from the sofa, setting aside his notepad.

Harry struck his most professional, courteous tone. "You too. How are you?"

"Well, thank you. Very well!" Gone was the squeaky voice in favour of a lower, more relaxed tone.

"You look it, you spruce up nicely."

Nathan laughed his thin and croaky laugh. More inhale than exhale, it had never seemed an infectious laugh to Harry. *There's the old Nathan I know.*

"You are too kind. How are you, Harry? You must be tired from such a long shoot?" *Still a stickler for my schedule then, yet he's still not as keen as he used to be. If I didn't know him he could pass for a regular guy making conversation.*

"Exhausted" Harry admitted. "Hey Nathan, sorry to have kept you waiting so long. Wardrobe malfunction at the last second you know?"

"Nothing to apologise for! All part of the job, right?"

"Exactly. Hey, what are you writing?"

"Oh, it's for a script I wrote."

"Really?" *Right on the money, Joanne.*

"Yeah, I'm doing the proposal now but the script itself is finished, all ninety-two pages of it" Nathan couldn't help but look a little pleased with himself. To Harry's knowledge the man he now seemed to be had never undertaken, let alone finished, such a project on his own.

"Very nice to hear! Good for you, Nathan."

"Thank you, Harry." He turned to a satchel bag on the sofa and withdrew a bound and laminated white document. "Listen, it'd be an honour for you to read it, if you have the time of course?"

Here we go. Harry managed a smile to try to ease the blow. "That's the thing Nathan, we're filming flat-out as is and still running into over-time every day. Not to mention the reshoots we'll need to do after…"

The warm glint in Nathan's eyes dimmed and his hopeful figure deflated. "Sounds like you need a new director."

"You're telling me!" Harry's chuckle did not help sway Nathan's darkened face. "Sorry Nathan, I'm just being a realistic…maybe another time when I'm not so busy?"

Nathan warily asked "Ok, so that's a promise?"

Do I have to sign in blood too? "Yes, I promise I'll read it when I have more free time."

"Alright...I guess that could work."

"A rain check it is then?"

"Yeah, a rain check. Anyway, I should be off Harry. This proposal won't finish itself." He put the script and the notepad back in his satchel which he slung over his head.

"Unfortunately not." Harry tried to be as chipper as possible to raise the mood. "Good luck, Nathan."

"Thanks" He stuck a hand out to Harry who shook it. "I'll be seeing you."

Chapter Two

The rain lashed down on Harry's car in practically solid sheets that never relented. It had started five minutes before he was to leave the studio, now he was thirty minutes into his forty-minute journey and was thoroughly sick of it. Night crept up quickly this time of year and it was pitch-black now, no moon or stars to enjoy due to the storm raging all around. Harry usually didn't mind the commute to and from the city, living in the countryside could offer him a quiet calm that felt cathartic after hectic days at the studio. At this moment he rued declining Joanne's offer of a lift to the pub, where most of the other cast and crew would be enjoying hot food, cold beers and stroking Bitter, the landlady's black Labrador, behind the ears. Bitter was loving and warm; what the landlady lacked in imagination she made up for in food quality. Harry could not help but remind himself that they would all be patting their stomachs and loosening their belts about now. *I'll be like that in an hour or so, then I'll be able to get that early night's sleep that I need.* It would inevitably lead to a late and boozy night at the pub, which had its charms but wasn't what he needed. He was thirty-seven yet felt his age upon him nonetheless over these past few years, the hangovers were worse now and left a deathly feeling that really didn't help when working, no matter how good the horror.

There had been a car trailing behind him for the past few miles, far away enough to forget for a while but whose distant headlights popped up in his rear-view mirror every now and again. The winding country roads and thick hedges often blocked any sight of another vehicle unless it was twenty metres ahead or behind. Harry knew these roads well but still didn't dare to break thirty miles per hour, the weather was unforgiving and he didn't fancy adding some hedge-sourced accessories to his hatchback. Light suddenly flooded his car and mirrors.

Harry didn't realise how close the driver had got until it came upon him in a couple of seconds. That reduced visibility to some very bright hedges on either side and some retina-punishing mirrors he couldn't escape. An angry blast of the car horn did nothing to deter the optical assault. *What does he expect of me? Overtaking isn't an option on these roads, does he expect to pass through me like I'm a ghost?* A sharp right turn in the road caught Harry unawares and he turned sharply to avoid the oncoming hedge. The car behind had no problem maintaining its current intimacy with Harry's vehicle, with not even a moment's respite from the full beams that refused to quit. Another few blasts of Harry's car horn yielded little more progress. His warning lights had no effect either.

The hedges on his left quickly relented to reveal a gravel-strewn lay-by of sorts, Harry seized the opportunity and indicated left as he pulled in. Gravel crunched under the hatchback's tyres and harried the underside with a thousand little scratches as he brought the car to a stop. The car passed by on his right and drove on with its headlights and speed undiminished for even a second. Harry watched the brake-lights follow the incandescent world that went before the strange car's path. *Two square, red brake-lights. That could be most cars. Looks like a 4 X 4. There's lots of 4 X 4's in the world.* He couldn't be any more discerning than that, certainly not enough to glimpse a number plate. Those diminishing red eyes with a crown of white on black would yield nothing more to him now. *What an arsehole.*

He arrived home five minutes later and pulled into the drive-way, leaving the engine running for a moment after parking. The light from his headlights reflected off the newly painted garage door and washed him and the car in the deep red he had opted for. He couldn't help but think of the lights from the 4 X 4 before, seemingly hell-bent to blind him from the country road. *This is a moody red, like his intentions.* Harry's gaze snapped away from losing his thoughts in the garage door to notice the front door of his house on his left. *It's scratched, deeply. They look like claw marks from some great beast.* Harry got out of his hatchback and walked closer. Shards and larger, curled strips of peeled wood lay around the doorstep. *Someone, or something, really doesn't like this door...or me. This night is turning stranger by the minute.*

Harry had no neighbours, the nearest was an elderly couple, Angela and Anthony, that lived half a mile down the lane. Even if they lived next door, their fondness for the bottle meant they would both likely be catatonic by now anyway. Certainly numb enough to hear little to nothing of whatever had ravaged Harry's front door. He looked around for anything else out of the ordinary. The wet gravel outside the front door looked a little scuffed but not suspiciously so. Harry squinted through the rain and into the darkness that swallowed the answers he wanted from it. *Who are you and why have you done this?*

Once inside his house, Harry stripped off his sodden clothes and hung them across a few radiators. The gas boiler whooshed and ticked as he woke it for its steady climb to that's-more-like-it. The kettle, almost eager to impress, boiled in half a minute and helped to relax Harry as he poured water into his obscenely large mug. *A big thirst requires a big mug, and a big mug like me needs some home comforts now.* While his tea was brewing he went to his landline house phone. As soon as he put the receiver to his ear he realised something was amiss. *No dial-up tone. The storm must have brought down the phone lines. Not difficult considering how old they look.* His mobile phone had no signal so he'd found a small, queer excitement in the idea of using the landline phone that was picked up that infrequently it should be considered ornamental. It had made him feel enjoyably old-fashioned to get through to the police on something that wasn't a mobile. He strained the tea bag, binned it and added a drop of milk to complete.

He was cut off from the outside world with only his home and cat for comfort, who wasn't even at home now. Shelley the cat was probably out hunting mice and voles, though he wished she wasn't. He always enjoyed the affectionate welcome home she gave him, despite her mainly wanting him for the food he served her. The thought of food made him realise how empty his stomach was. He scanned the cupboards, fridge and freezer to find a small pot of marmite, one red onion, half a bottle of blackcurrant cordial and a whole load of ice. *Not exactly a meal for a king, unless I want to get seriously experimental about it. Real good planning, Harry.* There was a convenience store in the nearest village, Hornby, that would be open for another thirty minutes. He could grab a pizza, some sauce for dipping and a few beers to wash it down with. Then he would have all he needed for a night of no more interruptions.

So back out into the night he went, past the door shavings, into his hatchback and out the drive. The rain had thankfully just stopped so everything outside the car was still drenched. The road glistened from his headlights and the hedges to either side wore fat water droplets that winked as Harry snaked through the country towards his lifeline for the night. He was glad the only light around came from his own car. Swerving into the gravel lay-by and the unrelenting headlights seemed like a bad dream now. A good brew had helped settle him some, but it couldn't calm the rumbling in his stomach. He felt an impatience grow inside him that yearned for a hot, tasty meal.

With twenty minutes till closing time, Harry pulled up outside Welling Stores, the family-ran convenience store that served all of Hornby. In fairness, two hundred and fifty people could find the basics they needed at Welling Stores with a weekly trip to Lancaster, the nearest city, for more specialised and luxurious items.

"Harry Bates, as I live and breathe!", Arthur Welling exclaimed as Harry entered the shop.

"Evening Arthur, not too late to pick up a few things I hope?"

"Not at all Harry my boy! I was 'bout to close up early with it bein' such a quiet evening. The rains drive most folk away you see."

"I know, fortunately it stopped just before I got out of the house. Almost killed me earlier though." Harry told Arthur about his journey through the storm and the driver that had harassed him.

"Sounds like one of them boy racers from the city playing silly buggers", Arthur replied once the tale was told.

"Could well be", Harry admitted. "Wish they'd play with someone else though."

"I hear you, Harry. What can I do for you?"

"Oh, yes. I'll need beer, pizza and mayonnaise."

"Well we've got all that. Check the new ales at the back, Wes has done a new brew that's very pleasant."

"Oh yeah?" Harry made his way to the back and saw that it was really only Wes' beers that were sold. *Nice little monopoly there, Wesley.* He tucked three bottles under his arm. "Do you still sell those fancy pizzas with the sourdough base?"

"Sourdough? Oh, yes. Over there." Arthur gestured to Harry's left. "I can't pronounce the names but there's a meaty one, a cheesy one and a veggie one. The veggie one never sells but they keep sending it thinking it's gonna fly off the shelves any day." Harry picked up the cheesy one, a jar of mayonnaise and brought everything to the counter. "Each to their own, Harry, but I personally never got this whole mayonnaise obsession that's going on now. What's wrong with barbeque sauce or good ol' ketchup?"

"Nothing wrong with them, Arthur. I just prefer mayonnaise."

"Fair enough. You movie types and your European habits. 'Egg sauce' I call it." Harry couldn't help but laugh.

"Your turn of phrase is something I hope I never stop enjoying." Arthur grinned.

"I aim to please, my friend." Harry paid up and turned to leave when he stopped.

"Arthur, my front door was attacked by something today."

Arthur frowned and blinked. "Attacked? What do you mean?"

"I got back from work and there were these deep...gouge marks in my front door with bits of wood everywhere."

"Well that's not good!"

"No it isn't."

"Do you think you could be overfeeding that cat of yours and she's got too big for her boots?"

"Unless I've been accidentally feeding her plutonium, I don't think so."

"If it's not her then I have no idea sorry...unless it was the Beast of Bowland Forest?"

"The Beast of Bowland Forest?"

"That's the one, it's not a full moon is it?" A pause fell between them.

"Oh shut up, Arthur!" Arthur cackled until it became a coughing fit.

"Almost had you then, Mister Hammer Horror!"

"I've heard them all you old prankster. You'll have to try harder than that!"

"One day you'll drop your guard and it'll be over."

"Well, until then I'll be seeing you Arthur."

"Nice to see you, Harry. Take care."

Harry couldn't wait to be home. The thought of hot food, cold beer and a warm house made him put his foot down on the accelerator as much as he dared. He knew the country lanes like the back of his hand so he cut some corners that weren't too sharp. Pulling out of a particularly tight corner, the road ahead straightened out and he picked up speed. Up ahead was a dirt track that ran across the tarmac road Harry drove on. Such was his preoccupation with getting home, he failed to notice the jeep approaching rapidly from his left up the dirt track. The jeep emitted no light but twinkled slightly in the periphery of Harry's lights, not that he noticed this. He almost escaped the jeep's advances were it not for its speed, causing it to clip the back of Harry's hatchback. It still made an almighty bang and sent the back of his car swinging out right. He tried desperately to regain control of his car, turning right quickly to compensate. A spilt-second later he was through the right-hand hedge in a muddy field, slamming on the brakes to bring himself to a welcome stop. *No peace for the wicked tonight then...*

Harry rubbed his neck after the impact had sent him lurching right before he had reacted and turned with it. He heard the rumble of the jeep coming up the road behind him. Its halogen headlights were now on, somehow surviving the crash, and they lit up the hatchback-sized hole in the hedge with a brilliant white glow. Harry got out slowly, closed the door behind him and turned to face the jeep. It stopped and a door was heard to open and close. A figure in black stepped in front of the headlights and through the hole in the hedge. It was impossible to discern anything about them because of how bright the light behind them was. "Are you okay?", the figure called out.

"Yeah, I think so", Harry replied. "Not sure if I have whiplash or not."

"Oh really?" *That voice is familiar.* "Let's have a look at it!" The figure started to walk as quick as they could through the mud towards Harry.

"That's okay, I just need a min-"

The outline of a cricket bat slid out from behind the silhouette, now held in their right hand as they approached. Ten metres away and Harry started to back away. A few paces back and the mud was so wet that it held his right foot as he fought to pull it out. The figure rushed the last few metres, raised the bat and swung straight at Harry's head. He instinctively raised his arms as he fell back, the bat connecting with his left forearm, producing an audible *crack*. Pain shot up his arm like hot needles stabbing him, exacerbated by the wet thud as he hit the ground. His right foot remained entrenched in the mud so his ankle twisted uncomfortably from the fall.

The figure was on him in seconds, their weight pushing Harry down into the wet mud around him. They shoved a cloth into his face and held it tightly over his nose and mouth. It smelt of intensely sweet alcohol. His muffled shouts did nothing to relieve the sudden assault and his arms struggled to get a grip on his attacker. His head began to swim, strength fading quickly. Before he lost consciousness, the assailant said "Sleep well, Harry."

So much for my number one fan.

Chapter Three

Circus music...I'm about to step into the funhouse. Nothing scary in there, just wonky mirrors, roller floors and a silly slide that gives you a static shock at the bottom. A snap to reality that left the otherwise wonderous journey on a sour note. SNAP. That slide won't quit. It's that sparkly, smooth finish they put on it, the sparkles build the charge and you almost fly out of-CRACK-Fuck this slide and fuck this playhouse.

SNAP. That light is bright. Not a funhouse, a lighthouse. No, this is real. It'd be that 4 X 4 if it weren't for that filament in the middle, that and there's only one of this light. This is a lamp and I'm sat on a chair with my arms and legs bound to it. No, my right arm is bound to the chair; my left is bound differently. A hand holds my hair so my face looks into the light above. My left arm throbs in pain and my right ankle isn't much better.

"At least your head is fine, Harry. No harm to those looks of yours." The voice from before spoke softly nearby.

"Nathan...why?" His eyes adjusted to the light and Nathan's face came into focus on Harry's right. The lone light above cast dark shadows across his face, the left side in bright white and the right in a deep darkness. Both eyes were in the shadow of his brow, a tiny glint just visible in each eye. A wide smile spread wide across his face that unnerved Harry.

"Oh you know...jealously of you and your work...anger at you making me wait...disappointment at you snubbing me and my script."

"Nathan, you hit me with a cricket bat and broke my-" Harry looked down to his left arm and saw it had been tightly bandaged and held in a sling round his neck. He could feel a splint underneath the bandages too.

"That was...excessive I know. You made me wait again so I think was angry. But I fixed it, look! I'm not a monster, Harry." He chuckled softly. The circus music played on, coming from all corners of the room. Loud enough to be heard but not enough to compete with Nathan's soft voice. It was the kind of tune that showed no sign of stopping soon.

"Excessive?! You broke my arm and sedated me you fucking psychopath!" That wiped the smile off Nathan's face, revealing shadows in his hollow cheekbones like deep dark pits. A crackling was heard- SNAP-a jolt went through his body. Harry's mouth clamped down as his body suddenly tensed. He tasted blood as he bit the side of his tongue. *This isn't the funhouse anymore.* Nathan withdrew his hand and Harry saw a taser crackling with blue-white lines of electricity.

"I understand your anger, I'd expect no less at this point in the story. But the language I will not tolerate, Harry. It's too easy, it cheapens what could otherwise be a good line of dialogue." Harry spat a globule of blood out to his left. He liked the idea of spitting it at Nathan but disliked the taser more. *I need to choose my words more carefully if I want to survive this nutbar.*

"Nathan...you're speaking about story and dialogue like this is a film." Nathan's smile returned, this time with pearly white teeth flashing and a silver, metal tooth cap shining like a star in the lamp's reflection.

"There are cameras and microphones hidden all over this room and others. Had you bothered to read my script you would've recognised this as the start of act two, after the build-up in act one."

"...That was you driving behind me with your high beams on?"

"Very good! Just a bit of light intimidation, my boy! You handled it well." *You could have killed me had I not found that lay-by...He doesn't care, this is just a game to him.*

"You attacked my front door too then?" That made Nathan frown.

"No…Oh, that. Yes, that was odd. A nice touch as it turned out but it was like that when I got to your house, I swear. I wanted you, not your door!" He laughed more loudly at that, moving out of the light and holding his stomach as he shook in tucks. After a moment he sighed, "A happy coincidence really, but not my design." Nathan moved back into the harsh white light. "My next step was to take your cat."

"…Shelley?"

"That's the one! She came straight to me, pretty wired actually but she let me pick her up no problem. She is *cute,* Harry!"

"How do I know you have her?" Nathan's left hand dug into his left jacket pocket, leaving the taser there he pulled out a remote. He pressed a button and the circus music stopped. In its place a heavily muffled meowing was heard. Harry's heart sank. Trying not to let Nathan notice, through gritted teeth Harry said, "Let me see her."

A cloth sack was taken off Harry's head and his eyes once again adjusted to the light. There was no harsh spotlight this time, this room was dingy but he could see more of it than the last. He had been cut free of the first chair, frog-marched into here by Nathan and tied up to a second chair. Nathan had tried to worry Harry by asking when Shelley had last been fed, given that she had received nothing during her time here at her new home. Harry hadn't responded to his goading, he knew what Nathan was doing and didn't want to give a reaction or anything to fuel another electrified punishment.

He could see Shelley right now, looking right back at him through the dirty metal bars of her cage. She was standing expectantly, her dark brown tail up and flicking the air occasionally. Her body hair was dark brown too, almost black on her back, getting lighter towards her stomach with faint vertical dark lines of fur covering her all over. Not that one could discern such subtleties in this dim, dirty, yellow light from the few lamps that lit the room. Nothing else mattered to Harry apart from seeing those round eyes with pupils as big as saucers looking back into his own eyes. He would do anything for her since she was his life.

Harry Bates had no one particularly close nowadays: no friends except those he had fallen out of contact with years ago; he rejected his colleagues' social invitations so frequently that it was only Joanne that held out in her unwavering attempts to successfully invite him for a drink after work. He barely spoke to his parents except birthdays and Christmas, let alone see them more than once or twice a year. It had been at least five years since he had been with a woman, longer still since a relationship one might call romantic. *I can live with all that, so long as Shelley survives this with me.*

Harry had almost forgotten Nathan until he spoke from a gloomy corner off to the right, jarring with Harry's train of thought. He stood cross-legged leaning against a large wooden table. "I've been trying to work out why you called her Shelley. Certainly not a sentimental attachment to someone past or present, as far as I can tell you're a loner...like me. No, it had to be something more obvious. I almost kicked myself when I realised who she's named after..."

"Go on then, Nathan. Don't leave me in suspense." He thankfully chuckled at that.

"Shelley Duvall! The Shining being your favourite film of course."

"But not for Shelley Duvall's part."

"Well, that's a given really!" Nathan's metal tooth winked through the gloom. "It's good to see you relax a bit, you can do comedy too you know?"

"Maybe I'll look into it."

"Not before your current project. Eyes on the task at hand, Harry." Nathan added reproachfully.

"What's the film then, Nathan?"

"It's a documentary horror and you're the protagonist." *I could roll my eyes.*

"...And if I refuse?"

"Shelley here will go longer without food and water. I could taser her cage. I could get her a much smaller home." He kicked a wooden box, not much bigger than a shoebox, a few feet towards Harry. "What do you say?" Harry looked back at Shelley who now sat with her two front legs up. She blinked at him. *We're both going to make this.*

"Okay…what's the scene?" Nathan pushed himself from the table.

"Well I'm glad you asked! So glad I think cute lil' Shelley deserves some water." Nathan walked behind Harry to a grotty sink on his left. "The reward for participation is nourishment, for you too Harry." Harry heard the tap creak into life and fill up two containers. *Positive reinforcement, Nathan? If you think I'll be your salivating Pavlovian dog then think again.* The tap closed and Nathan moved over to them, first he placed a bowl inside the cage where Shelley had moved right to the back. He then slowly poured a plastic tumbler into Harry's mouth, allowing him breathing breaks. "Better?"

"Yes," Harry admitted though he was still ravenous. *Fat chance I'll get something like that pizza now.*

"There may be more later, maybe some food, depending on how you do with this." He went over to Harry's right and dragged the large wooden table over. It rumbled as it moved over the concrete floor so Shelley stayed at the back of her cage, ears now flat and her large eyes on Nathan and the table. Nathan squared the table in front of him before pushing it towards Harry so the lip came to rest a few inches from his stomach. Nathan flicked a switch on the wall behind him and a spotlight came on above Harry so he could see the grain of the table and the individual notches it had acquired over the years. Five photographs dropped onto the table top, Harry immediately recognised himself in the top few he could see. *There's Joanne and me outside the studio.* Nathan spread them out as he softly spoke. "These photos show a typical day in the life of Harry Bates. You will arrange them in chronological order before time runs out." He pulled out a stopwatch and waved it.

"I'm being timed? How long do I have?"

"Ten seconds." *Fantastic.* "You can use your hands...well, your right hand." Nathan moved round next to Harry and cut his right arm free. He flexed it and rubbed where the ropes had rubbed with his left hand, poking out of the sling. "And go." *Jesus, man, no let up?*

Harry looked over each one in turn. Aside from the one of him and Joanne, one showed him stroking Shelley outside his front door "Nine..." Their shadows against the house meant it must have been morning, so he placed that at the far left. "Eight..." The next showed him speaking with Arthur at the groceries outside Welling

Stores. He never went there before work so he put that on the far right. "Seven…Six." Next, Harry stepping out of the studio doors. He put that just before the picture of him and Arthur. "Five…Four." Another, Harry at the pie shop. That went before him leaving the studio. "Three…Two." Last was him with Joanne so that slotted between Shelley and the pie shop. "One-that's it!"

Harry leaned back and breathed in deeply. "Well done, Harry! You get food for that performance, you do know your own life so well." *Just as well as you do, apparently.* Nathan crossed to the kitchen and brought over a bowl of dry food and a bread roll. The bowl went into Shelley's cage, which she set upon as soon as the cage door was shut. Harry picked up the bread roll and looked it over, turning it with his good right hand. *Slightly stale but should still be edible.* He sniffed it and Nathan laughed. "You have no need to worry, it's fine. If I wanted to kill you it wouldn't be via bread." That would put an immediate stop to Nathan's film plans, so Harry was inclined to trust him and took a bite. Nathan grinned back at him, "see?" It wasn't much but it was sustenance.

"Thanks. Can I get some more water, please?"

"Of course." Nathan refilled the plastic tumbler and placed it in front of Harry, who drank it straight away. Leaning on the right-hand side of the table, Nathan pulled the nearest picture towards him, the one of Arthur and Harry. "You know you're not that fun to follow, it's the same routine everyday." He gestured across all five pictures. "The weekends are even less interesting," his hand went into an inside jacket pocket and put down three more photographs on the table. "You just stay at your home and walk around the country." The three new pictures showed exactly that: the first of Harry holding Shelley at the front door, the second of him walking up

The Crag, a local hiking favourite of Harry's; the third of Harry dozing in the summer sun out in the garden. *These are at least a few months old. How long has he been watching me?*

"You know your own life pretty well...but what about a day in the life of someone else...someone like me?" He cleared the eight pictures currently on the table and swapped them for a new set of five. As he spread them out Harry saw that they all showed Nathan in some activity or another. "My cousin took these of me. Much better framing than mine, I have a lot to learn." Nathan chuckled to himself. "Ok go," he added suddenly, clicking the stopwatch. *Keeping me on my toes? Nice power game you have here.*

Harry's eyes scanned over each picture: Nathan at a desk writing, Nathan grinning and pointing to a pastry in hand, Nathan running in a park. The last could be a morning exercise so he put that far left. The fourth picture showed Nathan smiling and holding up the cage that Shelley currently occupied. *Shiny and new. How long have you had that now?* "Ten…" *That was never five seconds.* The last picture was of Nathan and, presumably, a bartender on the other side of the bar. While the barman wore a polite smile, Nathan grinned from ear to ear, metal tooth glinting and his glass stein raised high. "Eight." It made sense for him to visit the bar in the evening, so Harry kept that on the far right. "Seven…six." The pastry might have been lunch so he moved that to the middle. "Five." The run made sense to go first so he moved that to far left. "Four." That left Nathan writing second and showing off the cage fourth. "Three." *Seems like a sensible order for a day's activities, but this is Nathan.* "Two."

Harry put his right hand up, "Done."

"Alright, he thinks he has it with two seconds to spare!" Nathan clicked the stopwatch. "When in fact...oh dear, Harry." He made a tutting sound and moved the first four pictures around. "Only one out of *five* correct, poor show!" Harry kept shtum so not to give any satisfaction to Nathan, who pointed to each picture in turn. "It goes: pastries, pet shop, run, script-writing *then* a well-deserved pint. You really are self-centred, Harry. No one else matters to you do they?" The tone got to him.

"And how was I supposed to know if I've not been on your tail like you've been on mine?" Harry waited with bated breath for Nathan's reaction. He stared back at Harry for a moment, his face stone and unmoving. Slowly he slid off the table and paced away into the shadows.

He spoke quietly and deliberately, "because you don't have to follow someone to know them, you can just take an interest. After I couldn't see you because of that…restraining order, I was a wreck. Almost killed myself if it weren't for my cousin making me sort out my life. I started exercising and found a purpose again, to write this film…" Nathan lifted a wooden chair over to the table and, in one motion, spun it around back to front, swinging a leg over so he sat with his elbows resting on the back of the chair in front of him. "Once I had started with myself, I thought of others and realised that life is better with them. Like Liam here, he pushed the polaroid of him and the barman closer to Harry. "He's worked at The Hammer for eight months now. He likes thriller movies and thrash metal music. I learned all that from making the time for him, asking questions and listening. *Sure doesn't look that thrilled to be with you there.*

"Ok Nathan, I get it. I should have made time for you and your script…"

"Anything else?"

"Like?" Nathan's brow furrowed.

"Like the restraining order! I only wanted to work with you, to share the limelight with Harry Bates was my dream and you killed it!" Some of Nathan's spittle flew and landed on Liam's face.

"...I'm sorry, Nathan. I...shouldn't have been so drastic and should have given you a chance. At least I know now what you can do!" A quietly satisfied smirk appeared on Nathan's face. "I understand. Lesson learnt." The smirk disappeared.

"Not necessarily." *Flattery was worth a shot.* "You can't just say, sometimes you must do. Actions speak so much louder than words. Besides, it's a bit depressing here and we could both do with some exercise." *I can't keep up with this guy, mentally or physically.*

"What about my ankle, Nathan?"

"It's not *that* bad. Might loosen up once we get into the woods…"

Chapter Four

If I have to wear one more cloth sack after this I'll…I don't know what I'll do, but I won't be happy. The cloth sack was removed and Harry gathered his surroundings. He had been sedated before leaving the holding room so he tried to focus to shake himself from the chemical malaise. Sat in the back of the jeep, his bound feet rested on the tow-bar. The cool, clean, country air was a welcome change to the stagnant musk of the room earlier. "Welcome to Bowland forest, my friend," Nathan announced, gesturing with his arms and speaking with the pride of one revealing a personal project. Scrubland stretched out in front of them and sloped downhill, littered with ferns and bracken until it flattened out, maybe a hundred metres or so from the forest's edge. The scrubland was relatively well lit by the full moon, seemingly brighter than usual as it hung over the forest. The top of the thickest pine trees almost glowed like pale, bristly beacons in the moonlight, in contrast to a wall of black that stood below with just a few dappled, younger trees marking the forest's edge. *Of course it's a full moon.*

"A beautiful night, right? The air is cool, the moon full. Perfect for a hunt." Harry looked at Nathan, who had walked round from the side of the car to stand on his right. He had slung what was unmistakably a rifle over his right shoulder.

"What are we hunting?" Harry asked in vain. Nathan chuckled, "That's good, Harry. 'We'…" He cleared his throat and spoke extra clearly, "I will hunt you through this forest. This area of outstanding natural beauty." He gestured again towards the forest. "Your objective is to reach Shelley before I land a bullseye." He pointed to Harry's head.

Harry asked with a dejected inevitability, "and where is Shelley?"

"In the forest. You should be able to hear her though, she wasn't exactly at peace when I dropped her off." *I won't even reach the forest on this ankle.* "If you do reach her however, I do solemnly swear that you are free." He held his left hand up open-palmed with his right over his heart. "I'll have everything I need to start editing then." Nathan pulled out a knife and cut the bonds that bound Harry's feet together.

"This is the final scene?"

"Should be. Now, on your feet Mister Bates." *This will be the death of me.*

Harry shuffled out of the boot, putting his good left foot down on the ground and easing weight onto his right slowly. His ankle felt like it was on fire so he lifted it and rotated his foot, testing its flexibility. The further left it went the worse the pain was, nevertheless he edged off the car so almost all his weight was on his left foot. He brought his right down again and gritted his teeth as the pain returned. "Stand up then, we don't have all night." Harry said nothing since all his efforts were concentrated on letting more weight onto his right foot while holding onto the jeep for support. After a moment he let go of the vehicle.

"Walk," Nathan waved ahead of them impatiently.

With more than a little trepidation, Harry put his right foot forward and took a step, quickly bringing his left forward to rest on again. He let out a gasp as his ankle seemed to scream in agony. "Good. Another." Harry managed another hobble and grunted, trying everything to manage the pain. "Carry on, you've got plenty more to go." He grimaced through two, then three steps. "You get a head start before the hunt really begins...go!" Nathan fired the rifle above their heads with a bang that echoed off the forest. *Here we fucking go.*

Harry hobbled away at a fast walking pace, wincing every time he had to put weight on his right foot. *If I keep this pace up, maybe I can lose him in the forest.* "Go Harry, go!" Nathan called out from behind. "Your greatest role yet!" Harry would have extended his middle finger in reply if it weren't for the rifle. Fifteen metres away from the jeep, the ground became a lot softer, almost springy. It started to slope downhill now but came up in mounds of dirt here and there, presumably mole hills. Some were so large that he would trip and fall if he weren't careful of his footing. Making a straight line downhill proved difficult too since clumps of fern and heather were so thick that Harry had to navigate a way round them, weaving a path through. He tried to ignore the burning sensation in his ankle as he tried to maintain a steady pace, putting as much distance between him and Nathan as possible. Harry didn't know whether he would find Shelley, escape Nathan, or even live to see tomorrow but his adrenaline gave him the energy burst needed to find out if any of that were possible. *BANG.* A thistle flower exploded a few metres away. Harry looked up the slope and saw Nathan at the top looking down his rifle back at him. *Was that my head start?* Harry piled through a clump of tall ferns, hoping they would block Nathan's line of sight. He paused behind the ferns to catch his breath and rest his ankle, the pain distant because of the adrenaline that made him feel wired. BANG. A mole hill threw up dirt nearby. "Ballistic encouragement, Harry! No stopping now!"

Hopefully there would be some proper cover in the forest so he shuffled off, almost at the bottom of the slope now. Round a thicket, over a crater, through more ferns. A thistle scratched at his arm but he barely felt it, all that mattered was getting to the forest.

The ground levelled out and Harry allowed himself a look up and ahead. The forest seemed to eat most light that touched it, he hoped it would swallow him too. The tallest pines were easily eight storeys high and had an imposing, powerful presence from where Harry looked up at them. There was about a hundred metres to the forest's edge, he knew he needed to do that in one run, if it could be called a run. A few metres in and another shot hit the ground off to his left. "Go on, Harry!" Nathan called out from behind. The level ground made it marginally better for his ankle, allowing him to keep a steady pace as the forest loomed ahead. He almost reached the shadow of the trees until the ground dipped suddenly, causing him to fall. He made sure to fall on his right side, saving his left arm and the sling it was kept in. The heather he fell on cushioned his fall somewhat, *small mercies in strange times.* He heard Nathan hooting as he extracted himself from the heather and tried to pick up the pace he had earlier as he passed into the shadow of the pines.

Twigs cracked and snapped under his feet and he reached the first tree, hand on the crenelated bark for support while he edged round the trunk, putting it between him and Nathan. His shouts and woops sounded much more distant on this side of the pine tree, Harry thought as he caught his ragged breath. *This forest absorbs sound as well as light.* He squinted through the darkness to make out pine trees up to seven or eight metres in front of him, beyond that it was a murky black. *Hang in there, Shelley. I will find you.* Using tree by tree for support, Harry Bates hobbled into the gloom.

Moonlight penetrated the forest canopy less and less as he delved further in. He therefore found it reassuring when he reached the odd illuminated spot, a stark contrast to the deep and unsettling darkness all around. He always stayed on the outskirts of such beacons so he wasn't visible to Nathan, wherever he might be. Harry took a moment at every stop to rest his ankle and listen to the forest for an encouraging meow from Shelley and not a twig breaking due to a nearby super-fan. *If I don't see this level of hero-worship again, that is just fine.* He strained to hear any leading clue but the forest gave up nothing apart from the branches overhead rustling in the wind and the occasional creak of a tree. The wind didn't make it close to the forest floor so the air hung still; that and the hushed silence kept Harry on edge. Each footstep produced an audible crunch that felt much louder than it should be, fuelling Harry's growing feeling that it would lead Nathan straight to him.

He started creeping away from his current spot when he heard the crunch of twigs breaking. Another crunch. Harry realised it was a much louder, heavier sound than the one produced by his own path through the pines. The sounds came from somewhere off to his right. Harry remained frozen apart from slowly turning his head to get a view without attracting more attention. *Trees, darkness, a large branch on the floor, more trees and darkness.* He waited for anymore sounds. Nothing but rustling up in the canopy. He was about to move to the next tree when the broken branch moved. It strained for a split-second then loudly broke into two. As it broke, the darkness behind it seemed to shift, only for a moment but it was at least twice the size of Harry and a whole lot wider. A low rumble emanated from the black and Harry realised it was a growl. His heart skipped several beats. He thought he could just see the glint of moonlight in a pair of eyes that were dark as night, looking back at him in his silent terror. After a second another crunch was heard as it moved a step closer; one hairy, black, massive paw now just visible. It was the kind of black that, like the forest, absorbed all light so it was virtually impossible to make out any detail, other than the hairs at the paw's edge. Harry couldn't move even if he wanted to so it was with blessed relief that he heard a faint meowing off to his left.

No cat meows like Shelley does!

The paw quickly retreated and the creature paused. A moment later there was more meowing and the darkness shifted again, the eyes disappearing. Twigs and branches snapped as it moved behind the trees and away to Harry's left. He waited until the creature's sounds were diminishing before taking a few deep breaths. *I have got to get to Shelley before that thing does.*

More meowing from afar spurred Harry into action. He shuffled as quickly as he could through the trees towards the meowing. His right ankle was a dull annoyance to him, barely conscious of the pain because of his urgency to get to Shelley. He paused, listening acutely for her. Another meow to the right moved him on and on. Through bracken, round a particularly thick tree trunk, ducking under a low-hanging branch. He stopped again. More meowing but a lot closer. He saw a moon-lit area through the pines to his left so he edged closer, listening for anything or anyone else.

As he rounded a tree he saw a wide clearing ahead, bathed in moonlight. On the far side was a carry case with Shelley's unmistakable face just behind the bars of the door. Another meow cut right through him. He stepped out from behind the tree and into the clearing.

Everything seemed to slow down. Step by hobbled step he moved towards her as she stared back at him. He passed the middle of the clearing and she let out a little squeak, which he knew as affectionate. He got down carefully on his right knee and reached out for her as she moved to him – BANG – his finger exploded in blood and pain. Harry screamed in agony as he fell to his right, holding his maimed hand in his left. The pain was excruciating. Blood covered his hands in seconds. He looked down and saw that the third finger on his right hand was hanging on by a flap of skin. Bone and tissue were visible amongst the blood that oozed from the open wound. Harry sucked in air and issued a fresh scream at the sight. Curled in the foetal position and nursing his bloody hand, he barely noticed Nathan approaching from the shadows holding his rifle. Now without the leather jacket he wore earlier, he watched Harry lying there for a moment before speaking.

"You deliberated, rather than taking quick, decisive action to save her. For that and everything else, there is a price."

"You shot my fucking finger off!"

"Yes, that is a bit messy" Nathan replied as he peered at Harry's hand. "Oh well, time to finish the job." Nathan raised the butt of the rifle to his shoulder and looked down the barrel at Harry. Shelley started to hiss. "How touching, even Shelley knows how this ends. Any last words?"

Harry heard and felt heavy thuds on the ground. From behind Nathan an immense creature stepped into the moonlit clearing. It was so tall that Harry could easily see it over Nathan's shoulder. Even when lit directly by the moon, its long hair was so black that it was a difficult to decipher shape and texture anymore than a hulking, powerful body with four thick legs and an equally hairy head. The head yielded no easy definition except from a short snout like a bear's, long white teeth and those black eyes that held the moon in each. "Watch your back."

Nathan frowned and turned to face the creature. Harry could feel its rumbling, bassy growl through the ground. Nathan slowly raised his gun and fired at its face. It grunted in pain and stepped back. Nathan attempted to reload but the creature stepped forward and roared a deep, monstrous, primal onslaught on the senses that made even Harry forget about his mutilated hand for a second. Spittle flew at Nathan from its gaping maw before it brought up a gigantic, clawed paw and swiped at him, smacking him through the air to the other side of the clearing.

In seconds it had moved on him, thundering across to Nathan who barely let out a scream before its long white teeth had sunk deep into his torso, engulfing the top half of his body. It lifted him up and started to shake him violently from side to side, causing his legs to wave around like a ragdoll's. Harry stared, transfixed by the horror happening before him until he realised this was the time to go.

To the sounds of Nathan's dismemberment, Harry Bates got to his feet and picked up Shelley's travel-case, cradling it in his slung left arm and held in place by his disfigured right hand. Making sure to keep Shelley secure, he hobbled away from the clearing and into the forest. He used the patches of moonlight dotted throughout the pines to keep the moon behind him. It took a while till he couldn't hear Nathan's final scene anymore, the forest eventually swallowing that up too. After what felt like at least an hour, he saw light through the trees and emerged at the forest's edge. The pain and sheer exhaustion started to return as the adrenaline slowly wore off. Spurring himself on, Harry climbed the slope and sighed a huge sigh of relief when he spotted Nathan's jeep fifty metres away. It was mercifully unlocked and Nathan's car keys were in the jacket that he had left on the back seat.

Harry lifted Shelley's travel-case up onto the back seat and looked in. She stayed very still at the back, vomit scattered around the case. *Poor girl. The night she's had...The night I've had...We made it, Shelley.* Harry looked at the finger which still held on by a flap of skin, the tissue still raw but the blood flow had slowed significantly. *We keep holding on, girl.* He wrapped the seatbelt around her case, closed the door and slowly got into the driver's seat, closing the front door behind him. After a few deep breaths he turned the key in the ignition and pulled the jeep around, starting down the dirt track from where it surely came up.

He would gather his whereabouts and drive on to Lancaster Royal Infirmary. They would fix his right ankle, his left arm and hopefully reattach the finger on his right hand. After that some downtime was in order. It would be nice to see Joanne again, Mum and Dad too. He could catch up on his reading also, some light-reading first though. *That's enough horror for now.*

Printed in Great Britain
by Amazon